WRITTEN BY NICOLE HOUSENICK
ILLUSTRATED BY JANE COUNSELLER

IT'S ALL ABOUT SAM —OR IS IT?

SAM'S TERRIBLE DAY—OR BILLY'S?

Illustrations by: Jane Counseller

Balboa Press books may be ordered through booksellers or by contacting:

Balboa Press
A Division of Hay House
1663 Liberty Drive
Bloomington, IN 47403
www.balboapress.com
1-(877) 407-4847

ISBN: 978-1-4525-7396-0 (sc)
ISBN: 978-1-4525-7397-7 (e)

Library of Congress Control Number: 2013908338

Printed in the United States of America.

Balboa Press rev. date: 5/7/2013

Dedication from the Author:

I would like to dedicate this book to my Mom, Janet Rudy, who always believed in me and taught me what true love is. Also to my Aunt Jo, who became her voice of encouragement after my mother departed. To my magnificent children, Stevie, Hannah and Trinity, that no matter how I teach them it is their lives that continuously are teaching me. And last but not least, to my husband for whom no battle is ever to great!

Dedication from the illustrator:

To my beautiful grandchildren, Joel, Rachel, Chloe, Nathaniel, Johnny, and Benjamin. May you always be filled with peace, love and compassion. Also to my loving, caring husband, Casey...you all are my inspiration.

Sam was riding on the bus, coming home from school, when the incident happened. One that would ruin the rest of his day, break his heart, and give him much grief. Grandma had just bought him the video game the night before, and he was so excited to show the guys on the bus. Billy was sitting right near Sam, and here is how it all happened.

"Hey guys, look what I got!"

"Let me see", said Billy, as he grabbed the video game from Sam's hand. "This is dumb, who got you this stupid game? Looks like the game is as dumb as you look!" All the older guys on the bus chuckled at Billy's words.

Sam said, "It's not dumb, my Grandma got me this!"

"Who cares", said Billy, "Maybe your Grandma shouldn't buy you stupid things!"

Sam was sad and fought back crying in front of all the kids on the bus. When he got off the bus he ran home and as soon as he opened the door, he looked at his Mom and started to cry.

Sam's Mom looked at him, walked over to hug him and said, "What's wrong honey?" Sam took a minute to catch his breath and with as much composure as he could gather, told his mom what had just happened on the bus. Sam's mom felt a lot of anger towards the boy on the bus and she wanted to go and tell Billy to never go near her son again.

Instead, she said to Sam, "Well is it true?"

Sam said, "NO!"

So then she said, "If it is not true then you shouldn't listen to him. I think your video game is pretty cool, and I think you are the most wonderful boy in the world!" She gave Sam one last squeeze, and went off to start dinner.

Meanwhile........................

Billy got off the bus at his stop and walked home alone kicking stones gathered near the curb, along the way. When he got to the front door of his house, he took a key for the door out of his backpack. When he opened the door it was quiet and messy.

He kicked some junk, laying on the floor, out of his way and threw his backpack on the ground. He was hungry, so he went to look for a snack in the kitchen. He opened the refrigerator, and then slammed it because it had nothing he liked. He then went to the cabinet and slammed that too! There was nothing Billy liked to eat.

He walked to the family room and turned on the television. While he flipped through the channels, he could feel his stomach gurgling. He wondered if his mom would be home for dinner, or will she be working late again. Billy didn't know his Dad, but was sure that if his Dad knew him, that he would be there for him. Just then the phone rang. Billy picked it up and it was his Mom. "Hi Mom", he said.

Specials

"Hi Billy, I am just calling to make sure you made it home alright."

"Yeah, I'm fine. Are you coming home for dinner?"

"I hope I can, but I may pick up another shift here at the restaurant. There should be some tuna salad in the refrigerator and bread in the pantry, in case I can't get there."

"I hate tuna! Can't we have normal food like all the other kids in the world!"

"You know we don't have much money, I am doing my best. Just please don't complain."

"Maybe you can get me this new video game that all my friends at school have. It is really cool and everyone has one!"

"Billy! How many times do I have to tell you? We don't have the money. I am working so hard just to keep a roof over our heads. Be thankful that you have a warm home to sleep in. Those kinds of things are not important, you don't need them! Now go do your homework and I will call you later to let you know what time I will be home. I love you."

12
9
3
6

Billy hung up the phone without saying goodbye. He shouted as loud as he could, "I hate my life!" He sat down at the table and put his head in his hands and started to cry.

Meanwhile..................

Sam sat down to dinner with his family. His Mom made his favorite meal, chicken and mashed potatoes. Everyone ate, talked and laughed. It was a good night.

Questions to think about

1. How did you feel about Sam in the beginning of the book?
2. How did you feel about Billy in the beginning of the book?
3. What question did Sam's mom ask him when he told her what Billy said?
4. Has there ever been a time in your life when someone has said something hurtful to you and you did not know why? Have you ever asked yourself the question, "Is it true?".
5. Sometimes in life people say things that are hurtful and they are true. When this happens, do you think those people are trying to help you? How can you make yourself feel better when this happens?
6. When Billy arrived home, how was it different from when Sam arrived at his home?
7. How did you feel about Billy by the end of the book? Why?
8. Is the story all about Sam?

Note: I would like to thank a very special group of children who took the time to help with these questions. You know who you are!

CPSIA information can be obtained
at www.ICGtesting.com
Printed in the USA
LVIC052351220513
335028LV00002B